THIS BOOK BELONGS TO

....

GRAB YOUR COLOURING TOOLS AND GET READY TO COUNT! SPLASH SOME COLOUR ON EACH DRAWING TO TALLY UP HOW MANY ITEMS YOU NEED TO HUNT. HAPPY SEARCHING!

MERRY Christmas

THIS BOOK BELONGS TO

_____

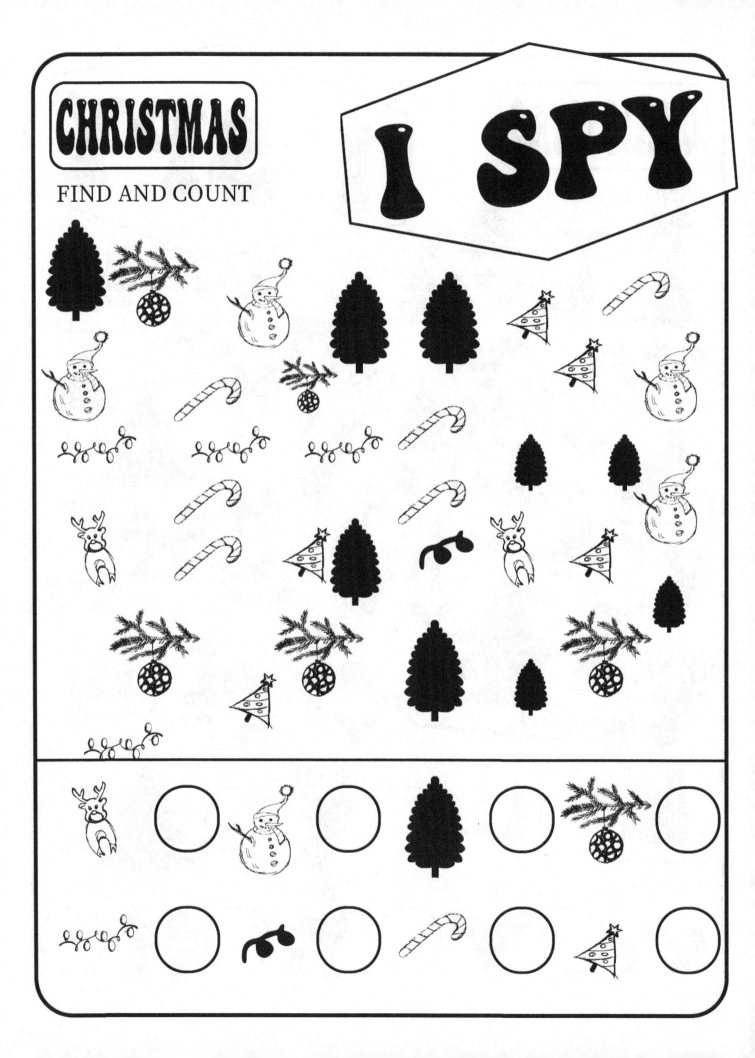

I SPY Christmas

Count each object and write the number in the box.

I SPY

FIND AND COUNT

I SPY WINTER FUN

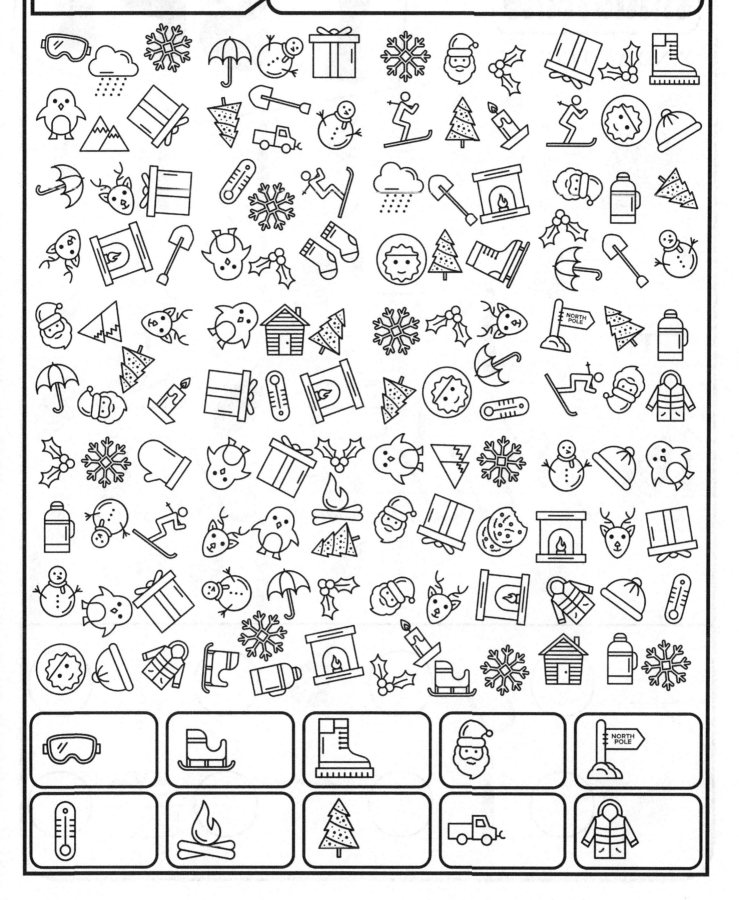

I SPY WINTER FUN

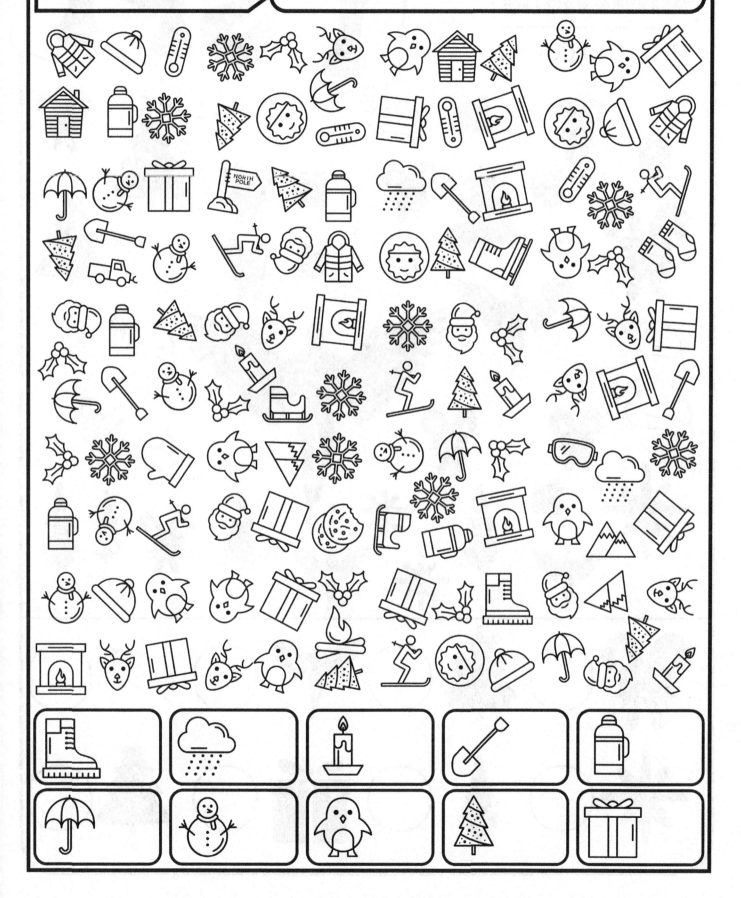

I SPY Christmas

Count each object and write the number in the box.

I SPY > WINTER FUN

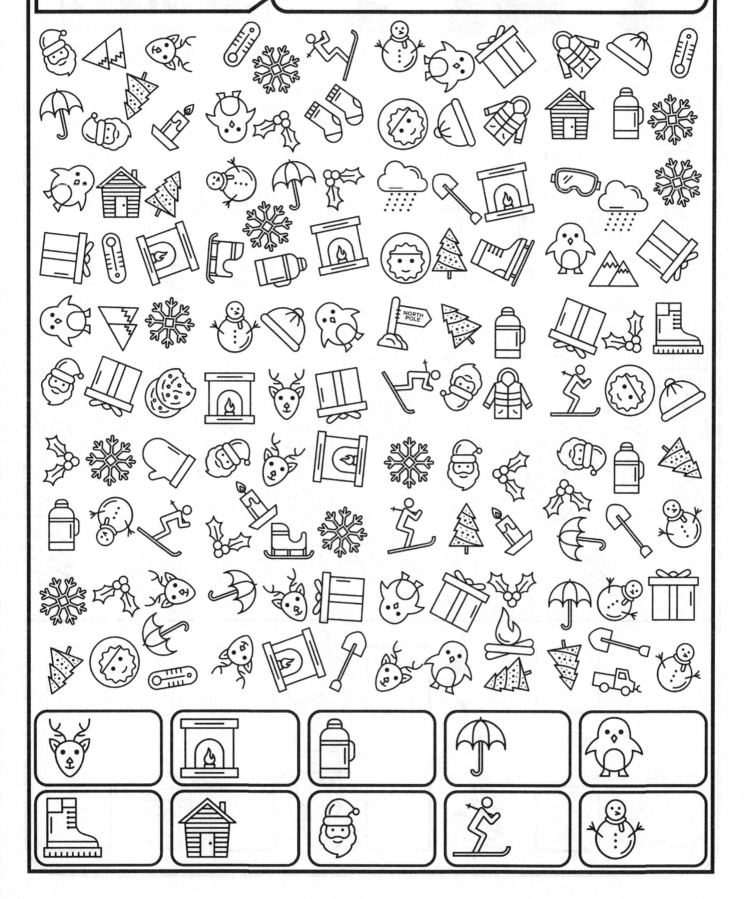

I SPY

CHRISTMAS

FIND AND COUNT

I SPY > WINTER FUN

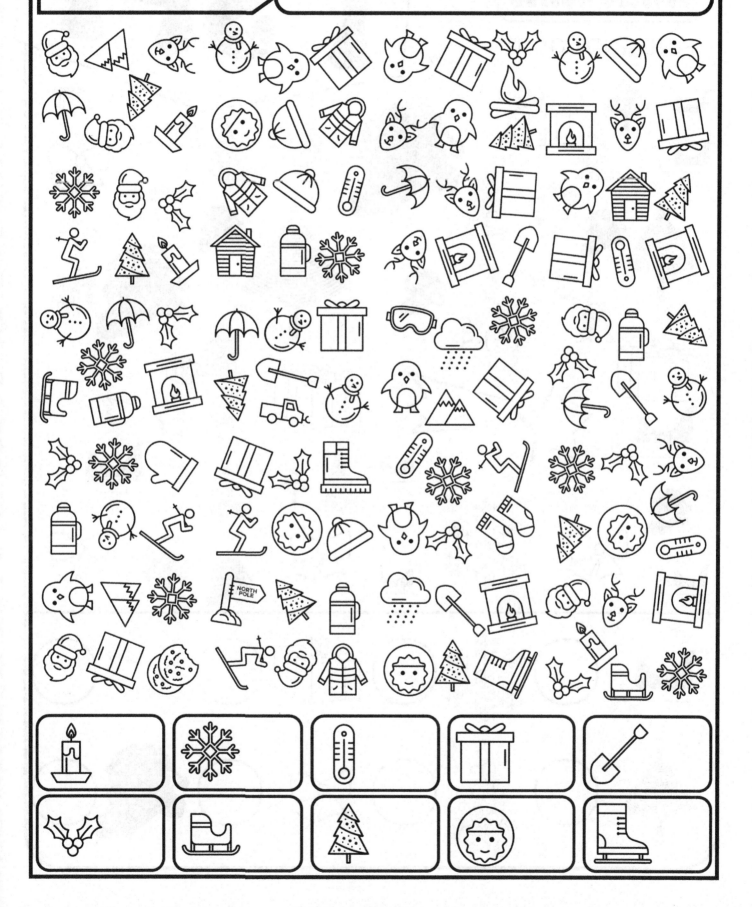

I SPY Christmas

Count each object and write the number in the box.

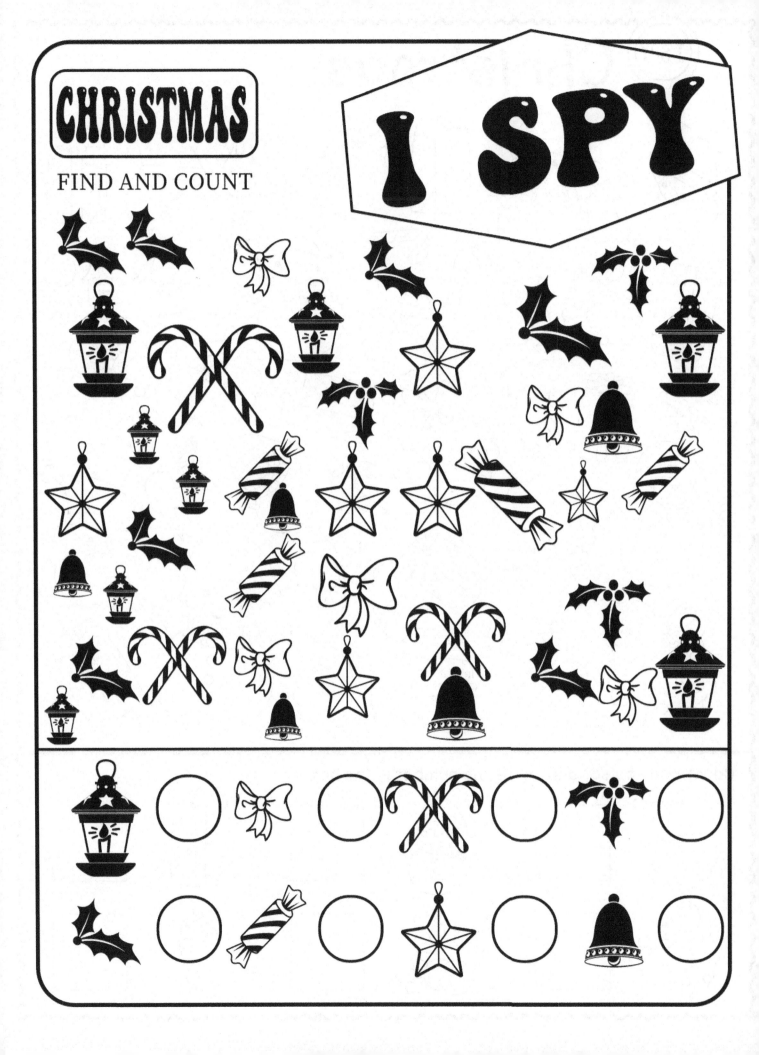

I SPY ▷ WINTER FUN

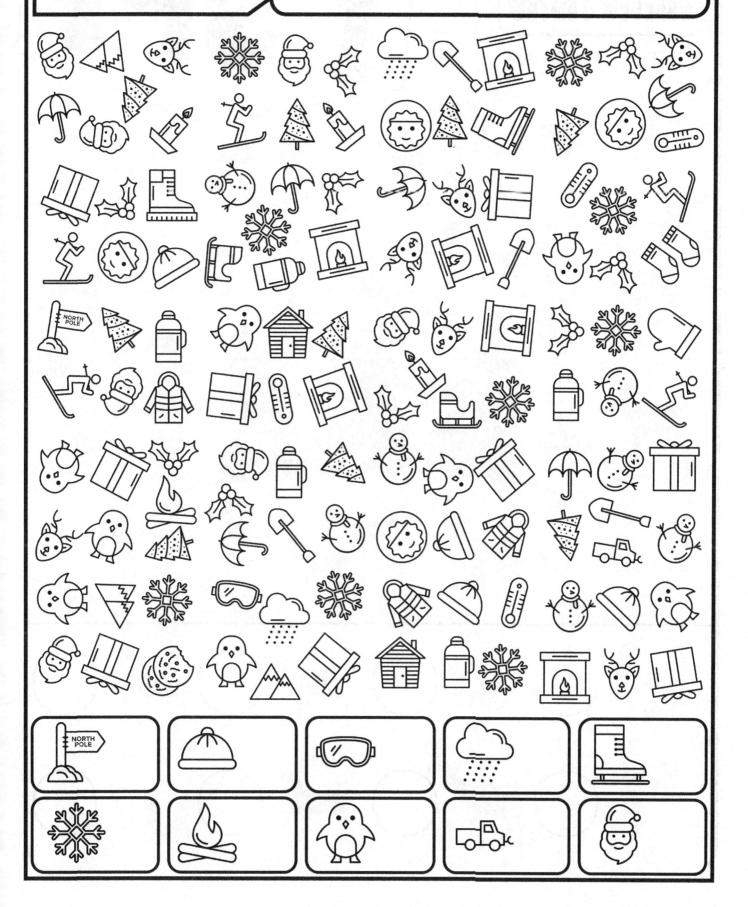

I SPY WINTER FUN

I SPY Christmas

Count each object and write the number in the box.

I SPY

WINTER

FIND AND COUNT

I SPY WINTER FUN

I SPY WINTER FUN

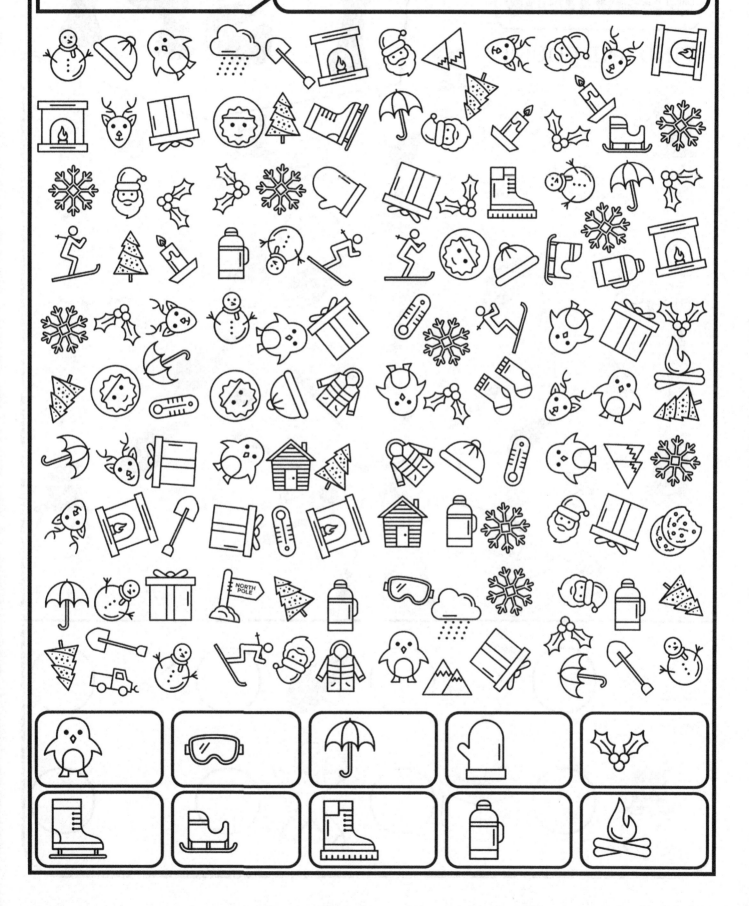

Christmas

I SPY

Count each object and write the number in the box.

I SPY > WINTER FUN

I SPY WINTER FUN

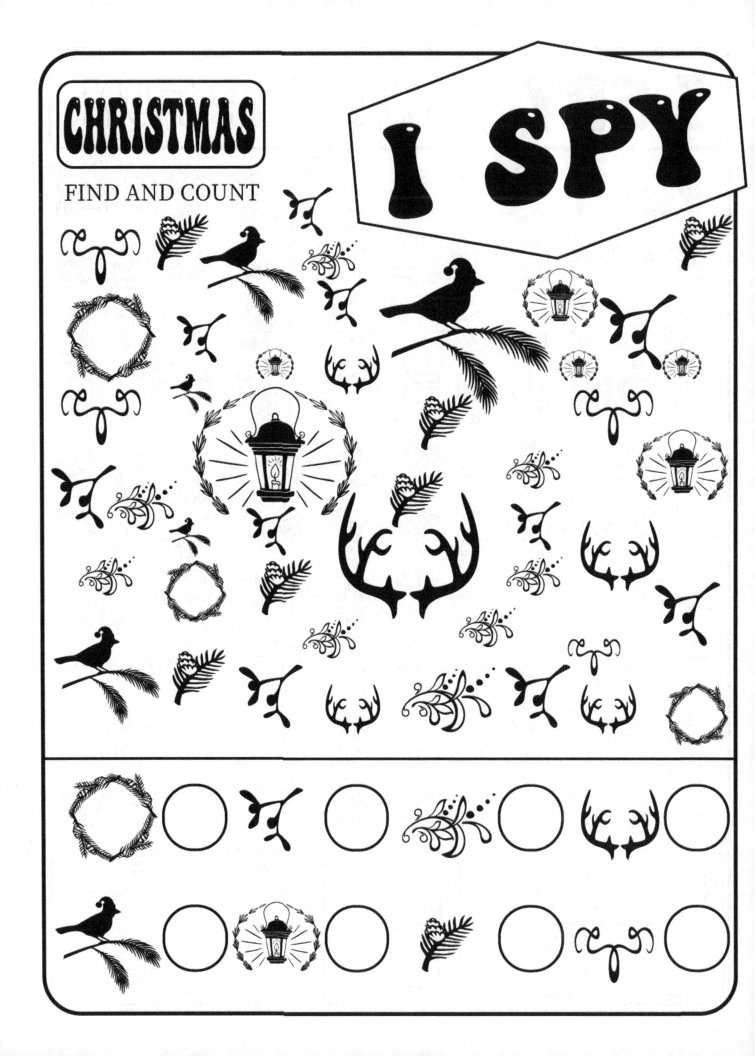

CHRISTMAS

FIND AND COUNT

I SPY

I SPY Christmas

Count each object and write the number in the box.

I SPY > WINTER FUN

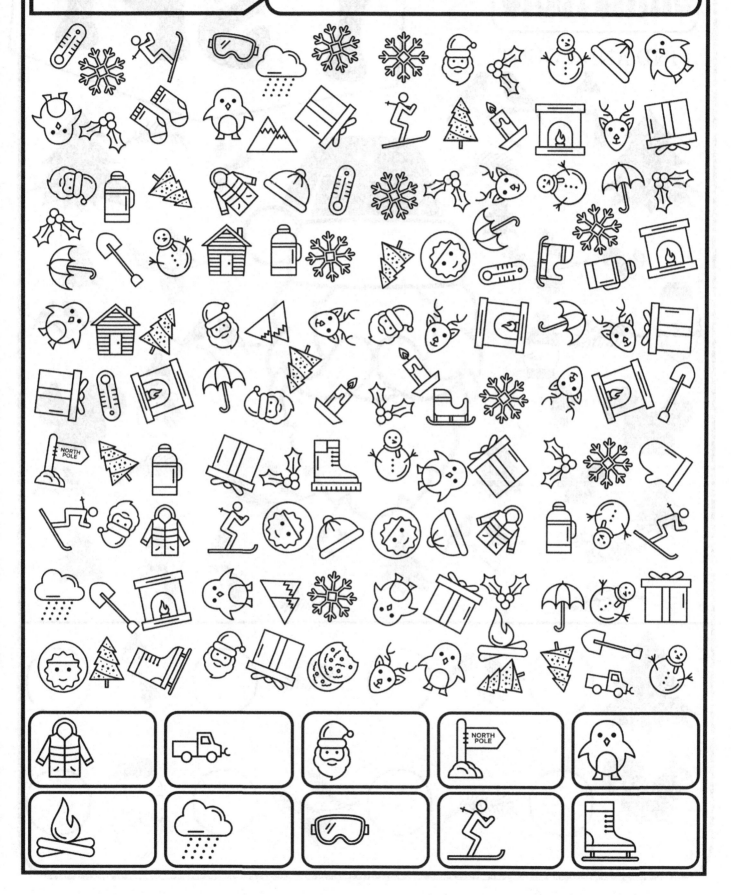

I SPY WINTER FUN

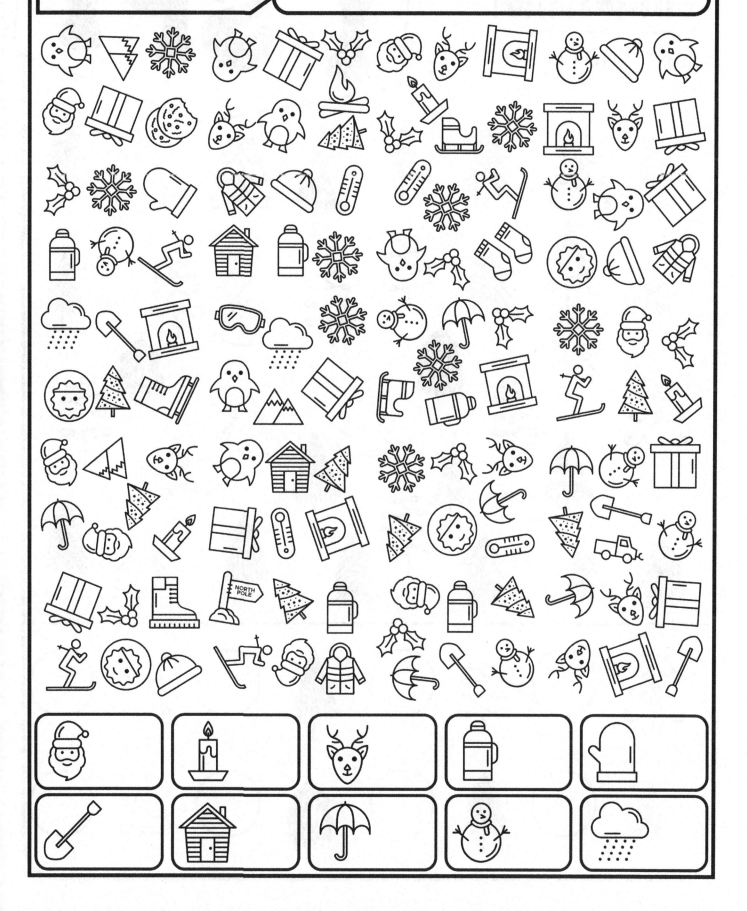

I SPY Christmas

Count each object and write the number in the box.

I SPY WINTER FUN

CHRISTMAS

FIND AND COUNT

I SPY

I SPY WINTER FUN

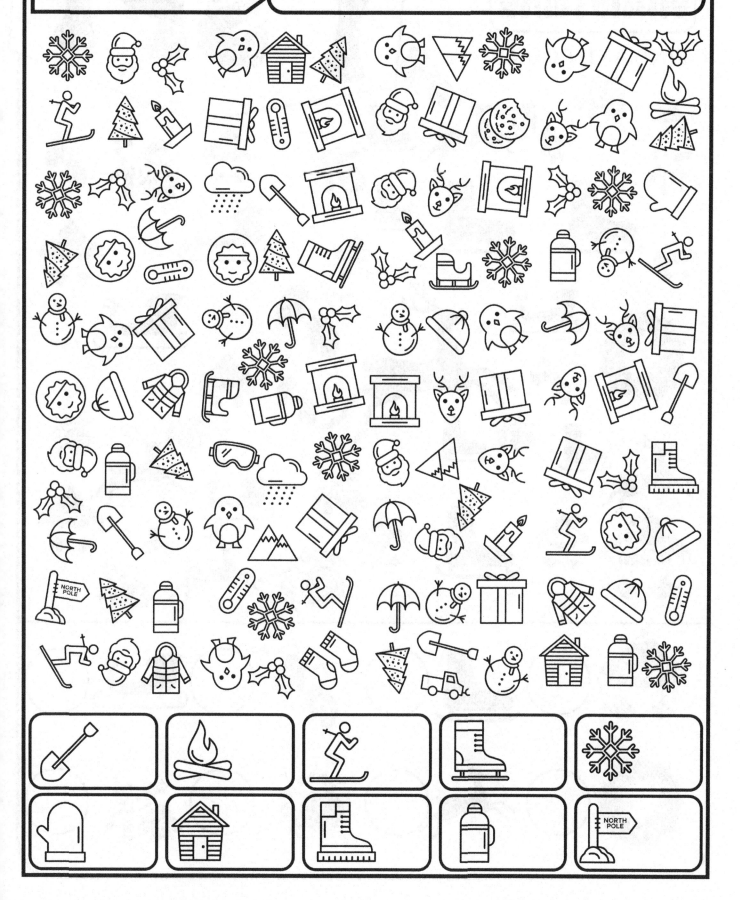

CHRISTMAS

FIND AND COUNT

I SPY

I SPY Christmas

Count each object and write the number in the box.

I SPY WINTER FUN

CHRISTMAS

FIND AND COUNT

I SPY Christmas

Count each object and write the number in the box.

CHRISTMAS

FIND AND COUNT

I SPY

I SPY Christmas

Count each object and write the number in the box.

CHRISTMAS

FIND AND COUNT

I SPY

Made in the USA
Columbia, SC
15 December 2024